Cody's
Secret Admirer

Betsy Duffey

Illustrated by Ellen Thompson

PUFFIN BOOKS

For Laurie

PUFFIN BOOKS
Published by the Penguin Group
Penguin Putnam Books for Young Readers,
345 Hudson Street, New York, New York 10014, U.S.A.
Penguin Books Ltd, 27 Wrights Lane, London W8 5TZ, England
Penguin Books Australia Ltd, Ringwood, Victoria, Australia
Penguin Books Canada Ltd, 10 Alcorn Avenue, Toronto, Ontario, Canada M4V 3B2
Penguin Books (N.Z.) Ltd, 182-190 Wairau Road, Auckland 10, New Zealand

Penguin Books Ltd, Registered Offices: Harmondsworth, Middlesex, England

First published in the United States of America by Viking,
a member of Penguin Putnam Inc., 1998
Published by Puffin Books,
a member of Penguin Putnam Books for Young Readers, 2000

1 3 5 7 9 10 8 6 4 2

Text copyright © Betsy Duffey, 1998
Illustrations copyright © Ellen Thompson, 1998
All rights reserved

THE LIBRARY OF CONGRESS HAS CATALOGED THE VIKING EDITION AS FOLLOWS:
Duffey, Betsy.
Cody's secret admirer / by Betsy Duffey ; illustrated by Ellen Thompson.
p. cm.
Summary: Nine-year-old Cody receives a valentine from a secret admirer
and tries to find out the person's identity.
ISBN 0-670-87400-0 (hc)
[1. Valentine's Day—Fiction. 2. Schools—Fiction.]
I. Thompson, Ellen, ill. II. Title
PZ7.D878133Co [Fic]—dc21 97-26812 CIP AC

Puffin Books ISBN 0-14-130565-7

Printed in the United States of America

Contents

Chapter 1

Junk Mail

Cody hurried across the street to the mailbox and pulled out a small stack of letters. He went through the pile one by one.

Bill.

Junk mail.

Bill.

Junk mail.

His parents got boring mail.

He had checked the mail every day this week. Valentine's Day was only two days away and to Cody, that meant cash.

His grandmother from Topeka always sent

him five dollars. His aunt Helen from Birmingham always sent ten.

In his mind as he flipped through the letters he started a list.

Top Ten Best Things to Get in the Mail

10. Letter from Granny (with cash)
 9. Letter from Aunt Helen (with cash)
 8. Letters from anybody

Cody's latest hobby was making top-ten lists. He made lists about everything. His notebook was full of lists.

On the bottom of the pile he came to a letter—a letter for him. His list was forgotten.

Who was it from? He checked the return address. There wasn't one. He checked the postmark. It was mailed from his own town. Not from Granny. Not from Aunt Helen. Who then?

He walked toward the house, his attention focused on the envelope.

Maybe it was his orders for a secret mission—just like on that spy show he watched on TV. He thought about the mail lady. She wore a blue uniform and always had her hair pulled back in a knot. She looked . . . well . . . like a spy.

He imagined the words inside the envelope. *If you choose to accept this mission, pull your right ear twice.*

Cody pretended that he was a secret agent like Double-O Seven. He pulled his ear twice. Nothing happened.

He turned the envelope over and saw a small heart sticker on the back. His spy theory vanished. Spies did not put little hearts on the backs of their letters.

He looked harder at the envelope.

Maybe it was a letter from the author he had written to during book week. Then he remembered Ms. Harvey had pointed out that his author was dead.

He sniffed the envelope. It smelled funny,

like his mother's magazines. It was definitely sent by someone alive. He sniffed again.

Very alive.

He carried the small pile of mail toward the house and went inside.

He stepped over his dog Pal and dropped the other mail on the kitchen counter. "I got a letter," he said to Pal. Pal didn't move. Cody walked on through the house, savoring his letter. It almost seemed warm in his hand.

His mother was up on a ladder painting the trim around the living-room ceiling. His father's best friend from college was coming all the way from India with his wife in three days, and Cody's mom wanted to make a nice impression. She had taken the week off from work to get ready.

"Hi, Mom," Cody called. "I got the mail."

"Thanks, Cody. One more wall and I'll take a break."

"I got a letter."

He shook the letter, then held it up to the light. He couldn't see through it.

"From Granny?"

"Nope."

"Aunt Helen?"

"Nope."

"Who's it from?"

"I don't know," Cody said. "I haven't opened it yet."

She dipped the brush again and reached way out to get the last corner. "Well, open it, silly."

He worked his finger into the corner of the envelope and tore it across the top.

He slid out the card. On the front was a large heart with a giant bee peeking around it. *Hi, Honey!* was written in big letters on the front.

He opened the card and shook it hopefully. No money.

Inside, big red letters spelled out, *Hoping you'll beeeeee mine!*

Cody stared at the card. His breath stopped suddenly. He had a lot of girl friends but he didn't have *girlfriends*. The idea made his hands sweat.

"Well?" said his mother. She paused from her painting. "Are you okay?"

He closed the card. Then opened it. The words were still there.

I <u>like</u> you. Your Secret Admirer.

"Who's it from?"

He couldn't answer her question. Normally the words "Who's it from" would bring him joy to answer, but not this time.

He finally found his voice and answered the best that he could:

"Junk mail."

Top Ten Things You Hate to Hear Your Mother Say

10. "Ask your father."

9. "Bring me the change."

8. "Do you have any homework?"

7. "Your teacher called."

6. "When *I* was young . . ."

5. "Let me think about it."

4. "You need a haircut."

3. "Don't spoil your dinner."

2. "What were you thinking?"

1. "Who's it from?"

Chapter 2

Double-O Cupid

"I don't know who sent it," Cody said. "I don't even want to know who sent it. I hope I never know who sent it." The idea of knowing who it was terrified him.

Holding the card, his best friend Chip sat beside Cody in Ms. Harvey's class. They were waiting for class to start.

"Man, oh man," Chip said. "It had to come from someone." Chip opened the card for the tenth time. "Did you notice the little heart over the *i* in *Admirer*?"

"Yeah."

Cody sunk in his seat.

"Did you notice that she underlined *like*?"

"Yeah."

"Twice?"

Cody put his head down. "I'm not ready for a secret admirer. I'm only nine."

"You should be thankful," Chip said. "In some countries people are married by the time they're nine."

Cody gasped. "That's impossible. No guy I know would ever agree to get married at our age."

"Their parents make them."

"What do you mean?"

"Like they pick out a girl for you and you're stuck with her."

Chip handed the card back. Cody slipped it into his notebook.

"So, who do you think it is?" Chip asked. "Let's make a list of possibilities." He took out a sheet of paper and started writing:

Top Ten Possible Secret Admirers

He paused. "How about P.J.?"

"I know it's not P.J. We're sort of friends, but she's always hitting me and kicking me and chasing me."

Across the room they could see P.J. arranging her school supplies for the day. She looked up and saw them looking at her. She stuck out her tongue and crossed her eyes.

"I don't know," Chip said. "My mom says that when girls hit you and chase you and kick you and stuff like that—that means they like you."

"Gross."

10. P.J.

"Let's see." He looked around the room. "Holly gave you half of her peanut-butter cup at lunch last week. Right?"

"But she said she wasn't hungry."

Across the room he could see Holly Wade.

Her curly hair was tied up in a ponytail. She smiled and waved at him. He smiled back

weakly. He liked Holly a lot but he didn't *like* Holly. There was a big difference.

9. Holly

"And Kate loaned you a pencil yesterday when yours broke."

"But she was just being nice."

8. Kate

"Let's get out our atlases," Ms. Harvey said. "Today we're going to learn about India. Remember that we're having a special guest on Friday. Cody's father's friend Mr. Avani from India will come to visit our class."

Cody smiled.

"Just think," Chip whispered. "If you lived in India you actually could be marrying P.J."

The smile went away.

Unwelcomed, the image of P.J. in a wedding dress popped into his mind. Worse, the image of himself in his Sunday suit appeared beside her.

They were walking down an aisle. P.J. was hitting him with a large bunch of flowers.

It was more of a nightmare than a day-dream.

The preacher in his nightmare-daydream asked, "Do you take this woman . . ."

"No!" he yelled.

Everyone laughed.

"Cody? I won't have yelling in my class!" Ms. Harvey frowned.

He nodded.

"Open your books to page twenty," Ms. Harvey said. Cody did not open his book to page twenty.

He looked over at P.J. She had raised her hand to answer a question.

"I'm going to solve this mystery," Cody whispered to Chip. "Just like Double-O Seven," he added. Already he was beginning to feel like a secret agent.

"Except you'd be Double-O Cupid," Chip whispered back.

Cody made his plans. At first he had *not* wanted to know who his secret admirer was, but he had just changed his mind. Not because he wanted to find out who it *was*; because he wanted to find out who it *wasn't*.

He took out his notebook and started a new list.

Top Ten Clues

10. Lives in this town
9. Has a purple pen
8. Dots her *i*'s with hearts
7. Likes to write letters
6. Writes in cursive
5. Puts stickers on things
4. Uses perfume
3. Likes bees
2. Likes *me*
1. Likes me a lot!

Chapter 3

Busted!

"Recess," Ms. Harvey called.

Everyone got up and hurried out the door. Everyone but Cody. He sat and watched the others leave. He watched very closely like a detective. Double-O Cupid. Softly he hummed the *Mission Impossible* theme song, "da da, da DA, da da."

"Do you feel all right, Cody?" Ms. Harvey asked as she put on her sweater.

He nodded. "Just wanted to look over my spelling words one more time. I'll be right out."

"Spelling words?"

"Yeah, I always like to do my best."

"Well." She looked doubtful. "I guess that would be okay. Ms. Wilson is right next door. I'm glad you're taking school seriously."

She left for the playground. Cody stared at his spelling words until he was sure that she was gone. Then he looked at his valentine. The little heart over the *i* had a happy face drawn inside of it.

He knew how he could find his secret admirer. All he had to do was check everyone's writing to see who dotted their *i*'s with a happy-face heart.

Cody waited until the sound of Ms. Harvey's feet died away, then Double-O Cupid made his move. He walked quietly to her desk.

da da, da DA, da da

There was a pile of English papers on the corner of the desk. He put his valentine down beside the papers and opened it so that he could see the writing inside. Then he began to look through the papers one by one.

The assignment was to write a Valentine's Day poem. There was one good thing about the assignment. Valentine had an *i* in it.

P.J.'s paper was on top. He checked the writing.

A Valentine Poem: Why I Love My Teacher
> *My teacher is sweet.*
> *My teacher is neat.*
> *My teacher is petite.*
> *My teacher has small feet.*

P.J. had gotten a check plus. Go figure. She had also written it in cursive. There was no heart over the *i*.

Cody's breath came out in one long whoosh. His secret admirer was probably not P.J.

He found Chip's poem.

A Valentine's Day Poem
I hate girls.
They are mean.
They are hateful.
They make me turn green.
Happy Valentine's Day!

Chip got a check minus.

Quickly he thumbed through the other papers.

He found Holly's.

No heart.

He found Kate's.

No heart.

Cody found his own paper.

I Love My Computer
Roses are red,
Pickles are green,
What I love most
Is my computer screen.

Beside the title was a check plus. He felt a

sense of satisfaction as he turned over the page.

He looked through all the others.

There were no hearts over any of the *i*'s. Cody sighed. Maybe it was just something that you did especially for valentines but not for English papers. That meant he couldn't rule out anyone—not even P.J.

He looked at the clock. His time was almost up.

He searched the card for more clues. It was signed with purple ink. His secret admirer had a purple pen. If he looked in every girl's pencil box . . . He moved toward P.J.'s desk.

da da, da DA, da da

The desk had two stickers on the top! The stickers said *A + student* and *I love school.*

Cody hesitated. He really shouldn't look inside someone else's desk. Ms. Harvey always told them to respect each other's privacy. But . . . He would just take a quick look in her pencil box. No harm in that.

He stooped down to eye level with the

desk. He could see the pencil box inside.

da da, da DA, da da

"Cody Michaels! What are you doing?"

Busted!

Ms. Harvey stood in the doorway of the room. The class was filing in around her. Cody still had a valentine in his hand. If he didn't get rid of it quickly, Ms. Harvey would see it. Everyone would see it.

He had to get rid of it. He did the only thing he could think of—he stuck it into the desk. P.J.'s desk.

"Nothing, Ms. Harvey. I . . . I'm looking for something."

"You're looking for trouble," Ms. Harvey said.

He spotted an old pencil under P.J.'s desk. It was only one inch long and had no eraser. It didn't matter. He was happy to see it. "Look, I found it," he said.

"Well then, get back to your seat."

He let out a breath as he stood up.

P.J. sat down and glared at Cody. Under

her gaze, he no longer felt like Double-O Cupid. He felt like Double-O Stupid. Double-O Stupid started back toward his seat.

Ms. Harvey watched him all the way. She was not smiling. He wished that he could explain things to her, but there were some things a teacher would never understand. He opened his notebook and began to write.

Top Ten List of Things a Teacher Would Never Understand

10. The inside of your desk is not really "a mess." *You* know where everything is.

9. Twinkies are a food group.

8. Heads feel better in baseball caps.

7. Pencils need to be sharpened often, especially during tests.

6. A person really can pay attention with their eyes closed.

5. Little League games *are* more important than homework.

4. Holes in clothes are a good thing.

3. Boys don't read books with girls on the cover.

2. Winning is okay—everything doesn't always have to be a tie.

1. Sometimes you don't look for trouble. It just finds you.

Chapter 4

The Valentine Kidney

Cody sat down. Ms. Harvey handed out white paper bags for the class to decorate. "Tomorrow is the Valentine's Day party," she said. "Tomorrow bring a valentine for everyone in the class and we will exchange cards."

Cody cringed at the word *valentine*. He thought about the valentine in P.J.'s desk. He thought about the words on the card.

I <u>like</u> you. Your Secret Admirer.

If Chip was right and his secret admirer was P.J., then everything was fine. He had given the valentine back and she would know that he didn't like her.

But if P.J. was not his secret admirer, then she would see the card and read it and . . . Cody put his head down on the desk as he thought about the words on the card. P.J. had seen him standing beside her desk. She would think that *he* liked *her*!

"Let's get to work," Ms. Harvey said. "These will be mailboxes for our valentines."

Cody felt his stomach drop at the word *mailbox*. He had to get the valentine back.

Ms. Harvey put the art supplies up on her desk. There was red construction paper, white lacy doilies, pink tissue paper, and glue. The kids walked back and forth from their desks to Ms. Harvey's desk taking pieces of colored paper and lace to cut.

"Did you find out anything?" Chip whispered to Cody as they walked up to the desk to get their supplies.

Cody shook his head no. Out of the corner of his eye he kept looking at P.J. She was cutting red paper into hearts. She measured each heart with a ruler to make sure it was perfect.

As Cody watched, she put down the ruler and stood up. She was heading up to the desk to get more red paper. Now he could see the edge of his valentine sticking out of P.J.'s desk. How could he get it back? If he walked slowly past her desk and bent down to tie his shoe, maybe he could grab it.

He quickly turned around and ran right into Holly.

Holly smiled at him. "Excuse me," she said. He noticed that the red ribbon on her ponytail had small white hearts on it.

His heart stopped beating. He couldn't move. He had actually touched a girl. Normally this wouldn't have bothered him. But now every girl was a possible secret admirer.

He watched as Holly walked on by. As he watched, P.J. returned to her desk. He had missed his chance.

What if his secret admirer was Holly? After all, she *had* given him half of her peanut-butter cup. She was the nicest girl in the third grade. But . . .

He had watched enough old movies with his mother to know what happened in romances. First you like each other. Then you hate each other. Then you really like each other. Then you really hate each other. Then you get married.

He wasn't ready for that.

He tried to think of something he could say to Holly to find out if she was it. He would be able to tell by how she reacted to the words whether or not she was the one.

He watched Holly selecting her paper at the teacher's desk.

What could he say? The words on the front of the card said *Hi, Honey!* He couldn't say that!

Inside it said *Hoping you'll beeeee mine.* He might get in worse trouble if he said those words.

On the front it had a bee. Suddenly he knew what he could say.

He hurried up to the teacher's desk and stood beside Holly. He pretended to look at the paper.

He leaned forward to her ear.

"*Bzzzz*," he said.

Holly swatted her hair as if she were shooing away a mosquito. She picked out a sheet of heart stickers.

"*Bzzzz*," he said again.

She swatted again.

"BZZZZZZZZZZ!"

She turned around.

"Are you buzzing?" she said in a puzzled voice.

Cody turned red.

"Just clearing my throat," he said.

She was not the one.

Cody sat down.

He started working on his bag to take his mind off P.J. and the valentine. He wrote on the top of his bag, *My heart belongs to you.*

He cut out a heart for his bag. The heart was lopsided. It was the saddest looking heart that he had ever seen.

He tried to even up the sides of the heart,

but now it looked like the kidney that they had studied in science. He glued the kidney-heart on the bag.

My heart belongs to you. He marked out the word *heart* and wrote *kidney*.

My kidney belongs to you.

He drew a little cupid beside the kidney. The cupid looked like an old man.

"What does Valentine's Day mean?" Ms. Harvey asked the class.

"Love," Angel said.

"Cards," Evan said.

"Candy," Chip said.

"Ewwwww," P.J. said. Cody saw her reading the card. The next thing he knew she was passing the valentine back to him. Everyone read it as it went by. Then they all looked at P.J. and then at Cody.

When he got the card back, there was a note in it: *If you ever say that again I'll beat you up.*

P.J. was not his secret admirer. But now

everyone thought that *he* was *her* secret admirer.

They were all staring. Cody squeezed his eyes shut. If he held them closed long enough, maybe the kids would stop looking at him. He opened one eye. Forty-six eyes stared back.

He looked down at his valentine kidney and frowned. Valentine's Day meant one thing to him: trouble.

Top Ten List of Things That Cause Trouble

10. War
9. Earthquakes
8. Tornadoes
7. Parent-teacher conferences
6. Water balloons
5. Report cards
4. Silly string
3. Pop quizzes
2. Stomach viruses
1. Valentines

Chapter 5

"Burp"

As soon as Cody got home he stood in front of
the bathroom mirror. He stared at his reflec-
tion. He hadn't realized that he had so many
freckles.

He imagined that he was a movie star like
the ones he saw in the magazines at the check-
out line in the grocery store.

They always had lots of girls around them.
They'd probably started with one secret admirer, just like him. He frowned.

It probably started like this, the road to
adulthood. First a card. Then a date. Then
marriage!

Cody wet his hair and brushed it back. It popped up again. He put on his baseball cap. It was a lot easier than making his hair stay down.

"Cody."

His mother knocked on the bathroom door. "Are you okay in there?"

"Be right out," he said.

"Cody, I need to put these towels in for Sunda and Stacy."

Cody opened the door. His mother hurried in and started arranging the towels on the counter.

"When will they be here?"

"Tomorrow night," his mother said. She fluffed the towels one more time and took a bag of dried smelly petals out of a drawer.

"Are you excited about Sunda coming to visit your class on Friday?"

Cody nodded. "Does he wear a turban? Does his wife wear a sari?"

"Yes, Sunda wears a turban. And Stacy

wears a sari sometimes, to dressy parties." She shook the dried pieces of flowers into a brass bowl. They smelled like cinnamon. "She showed me one once. It was beautiful. Some of them are made with real gold thread. When they get old, they melt down the thread to keep the gold. Sunda is bringing one to show your class."

"Cool," said Cody. "Will they bring me something from India?"

"Yes." She smiled and started to speak, then stopped. "No, it's a surprise. I promised I wouldn't tell you."

Cody turned to look at his mother.

"What? What are they bringing me?"

"Something special."

"What? What's special?"

"Oh," she said. "Nothing. Just forget that I said anything."

"Mom, I hate it when you do that. Something special is not nothing."

"You'll have to wait till Friday," she said.

"Mo-om."

"Don't whine." She pushed him out of the bathroom.

"Are you sure you can't tell me about the surprise?"

She laughed. "It wouldn't be a surprise if I told you. But I have another surprise for you, Cody, a small one. I bought your valentines for you today. Meet me in your bedroom."

She brought out a brown paper bag and dumped the contents on the bed. "Here you go. Valentines for all of your classmates."

Cody looked at the pile of valentines. Big Bird stared out from the packs of cards. "You got me Big Bird valentines?"

"They're cute," his mother said. "And I remember how much you always loved Big Bird."

"Thanks," Cody said. "I guess." As his mother left the room, he shook his head. He hadn't thought about Big Bird since kindergarten.

He sat on his bed and spread out the cards.

Big Bird was everywhere. His bed was a sea of yellow. He took out a list of names that Ms. Harvey had given them. On the white envelopes he wrote the names of everyone in his class. On the back of the valentines he wrote his name. On one of the cards it looked like Big Bird should be saying something, so Cody drew a speech bubble out of Big Bird's mouth and wrote, "Burp."

He gave that one to Chip.

He took out another card and drew another speech bubble. This one would be for P.J. He wrote in the bubble, "I don't like you." That sounded mean. He erased it. It might make her even madder.

What else could he say? *I'm not in love with you* sounded too grown up. He picked up his pencil. "I'm not in like with you," he wrote.

He tucked the card into the envelope with "P.J." written on the front. That should do it.

As he stuffed the valentines into the envelopes, he wondered which one of them his secret admirer would receive.

Most of all he kept wondering about his surprise. What could Sunda and Stacy be bringing from India for him?

He tried to remember the last time he'd gotten a surprise. He'd had a pop quiz last week, but that was a bad surprise. He made a list of all the surprises that he had never gotten. This one should be great.

Top Ten Best Surprises I Have Never Gotten

10. A trip around the world

9. A million dollars

8. A silver Lamborghini

7. 100 on a spelling test

6. A ride in a limo

5. A swimming pool

4. 100 on any test

3. Straight A's

2. Free tickets to the World Series

1. Something from India

Chapter 6

Attack of the Killer Valentines

"I heard that you like P.J.," Angel said. It was Valentine's Day and they were clearing off their desks for the party. "Do you?"

Cody's mouth fell open. It was the tenth time he had been asked, but the question still left him speechless. Everytime he saw P.J. she held up her fist. Romance was dangerous.

He longed for the day to be over. He had learned to hate valentines.

"Party time!" Ms. Harvey said finally.

Some parents came in with red punch and heart-shaped cookies. There were napkins with hearts and cups with hearts and plates with hearts. Red hearts were everywhere.

Cody had never noticed before in the picture on the wall how much George Washington's face was shaped like a heart. And the map of India. How could he not have noticed that the country of India was shaped almost like a heart! He looked at the hole in the knee of his jeans—heart shaped!

It was like a horror movie that he had seen about the attack of the killer spiders.

First there were none. Then one lone spider crawled across the screen. Then two. Then suddenly hundreds attacked. Valentines were like that—small and lethal.

Attack of the Killer Valentines.

He opened his book bag.

Yikes. More valentines.

"Hey." Chip tapped Cody on the shoulder. Cody jumped. "You know who it is yet?"

"Who?"

"You know. The *you-know-who*."

Cody shook his head. "Don't remind me," he said. He didn't want to think about P.J. and the valentine.

There was a lot of noise in Ms. Harvey's room. Kids were happily putting valentines into the decorated bags. P.J.'s valentines were packs of M&M's. Angel's were in pink envelopes.

He delivered his own Big Bird valentines, one into each bag. He thought about the message that he had written on P.J.'s card. When he passed his own bag he peeked in at the pile of envelopes growing bigger inside. He shuddered. Was there another one in there from *her?*

During the whole party, Cody watched his valentine bag and wondered about the cards inside.

Finally the bell rang and school was over. As everyone left, Ms. Harvey handed out the bags.

Cody walked out of the school with Chip. Chip started rooting through his bag until he found the pack of M&M's on the bottom.

Cody found his pack, and they ate M&M's as they walked.

"Don't eat the green ones," Chip said. He carefully shook out all the green ones and put them in his pocket.

"Why?" Cody asked.

"Every time you eat a green one you have to kiss a girl."

Cody spit out a mouthful of M&M's. They landed with a splat on the sidewalk.

Chip shook his bag. "The first thing we do is count 'em," he said. They sat down on the steps. "You first." Cody emptied out his bag onto the top step.

Cody counted his valentines, dropping them one by one back into a pile beside the white paper bag. "Twenty-one," he counted, "twenty-two, twenty-three."

Cody turned the bag over and shook it. He looked into it and felt down to the bottom.

"Hmm," he said.

"What's wrong?" Chip asked.

"I only got twenty-three valentines."

"So?"

"So. . . . There are twenty-four people in Ms. Harvey's class. Someone did not give me a valentine. That must mean that someone doesn't like me."

"I thought you didn't like valentines," Chip said.

Cody frowned. He had been so afraid that someone *would* like him that he had never considered the possibility that someone *wouldn't* like him. He couldn't decide which was worse.

"It's probably P.J.," he said.

"Nope," said Chip. "You got M&M's. That's what P.J. gave."

"Angel?"

"Nope. You got a pink one."

"Maybe I counted wrong," he said hopefully. He picked up the little pile of valentines and counted them one more time. "Twenty-three," he said in a sad voice. Cody put his head in his hands.

"Look," Chip said. "I have a list of everyone in Ms. Harvey's room. We'll take the valentines one by one and mark the names off the list. Then you can see whose name is left, and you'll know who it is."

Chip got out a pencil. "Go ahead," he said.

Cody looked at the little pile of envelopes, then picked one up.

"Holly," he said.

Chip marked off Holly, and Cody dropped the card into the bag.

"Evan," Cody read.

Chip marked off Evan.

"P.J." He held up the half-empty bag of M&M's. Then he picked up another card.

"Sue."

"John."

"Dalila."

One by one Chip marked off the names until there was only one name left.

"I know who it is," said Chip. "Man, this is great."

"Don't tell me," said Cody. "I don't want

to know after all. I mean I thought I did, but now I don't know. I mean—"

"Cody."

"What?"

Chip laughed. "Cody is the last name. You didn't send a valentine to yourself."

Cody's face turned red.

"I knew that," he said. He began to gather up his books. "Of course I knew that."

"Right," said Chip.

They held their bags and ate the M&M's, saving the green ones.

Cody put his valentines back in his bag. They didn't seem so bad now.

Top Ten Things That I Like, But I Don't Want to Admit That I Like

10. Social studies videos
9. Broccoli
8. Kisses from my mom
7. Cold pizza for breakfast
6. My old blanky
5. Snuffleupagus
4. Square dancing in gym class
3. Beanie Babies
2. Smiley faces on my papers
1. Valentines

Chapter 7

The Speed of Light

Cody saw the mail truck rounding the corner as he walked home from school. He slowed down.

He stood for a minute beside the mailbox wondering about his secret admirer. The best thing about secret admirers, he decided, was that they were secret.

Could he spend his whole life avoiding romance? Was avoiding romance as easy as avoiding green M&M's and the mailbox?

He eased the mailbox door open. There

was a small pile of letters. They looked harmless enough.

His flipped through the stack. No envelopes with hearts. He breathed a sigh of relief as he walked back into the house.

There was a letter from Sunda. He remembered about his surprise. Sunda was coming in late tonight. Tomorrow was the big day.

Cody smiled as he walked toward the house. Tomorrow Sunda would come to his class and he would get his surprise from India.

Cody held the letter up to the light as he walked back toward the house. He had the feeling that there was something important in the letter, and it was something that had to do with him.

He thought about the surprise and the way his mother had said, "Oh, nothing." He had to find out what was in the letter.

He looked harder at it. It was barely sealed. If he put his finger just under the flap and put a little pressure . . . The flap popped open.

Cody stared at the letter. It wouldn't hurt to read it. He would slip it right back. No harm done.

Dear Susan and Paul,
We can't wait to see you.
We're bringing Sita for Cody. He will love her. She will be a great addition to the family. We'll bring the necessary license when we come. See you Thursday.

Sunda

Bringing Sita? For Cody? Cody stared down at the letter in his hand. He remembered Chip telling him about how parents set up marriages in other countries. India was one of those countries!

Great addition to the family?

Necessary license?

Cody fell into a heap beside the front porch.

He was traveling into adulthood at the

speed of light. He was like a traveler on the starship *Enterprise,* but instead of zooming through outer space he was zooming through the years of his life.

One day a secret admirer, and the next— marriage. He had never even been on a date. By this weekend he would be a married man. A married boy?

Top Ten Reasons I Can't Get Married This Weekend

10. Married guys don't have Tigger sheets.

9. My allowance is not big enough for two.

8. I still like my mom and dad to tuck me in.

7. My hands sweat when I'm around girls.

6. They don't make wedding rings small enough for me.

5. Married guys can't play Nintendo.

4. You can't take a wife to summer camp.

3. My Sunday shoes are too small and you can't get married in sneakers.

2. Married guys know how to write in cursive.

1. I don't know how to hold hands. Where does the thumb go?

Chapter 8

Just Say No

Cody slipped the letter back into its envelope and put the pile of mail down on the kitchen table. He walked toward his room.

He thought about all the programs that the police did in his school. *Just say no to drugs.*

He thought of a new slogan: *Just say no to marriage.*

He had seen a zombie in an old movie. The zombie couldn't feel or see and kept walking into walls and doors. No matter what anyone said to it, the zombie could only say "Uhhhh!" Cody felt like that.

He walked past his mother without speaking. He walked into the side of the doorway to his room, then turned and walked into the room.

"Cody, do you feel okay?"

"Uhhhhh!" he said.

"Cody?"

"Uhhhh!"

He sat on the bed.

His mother came in and looked at him. "You're acting so strange. Is there something that you want to talk about?"

He wanted to ask her about the letter, but he didn't want to admit that he had read it. He tried to think of a way to ask her about it. He gave up.

"I know about Sita," he said finally. He waited for his mother to deny it. To tell him it wasn't true.

"You do?" His mother sounded disappointed. "We wanted it to be a surprise. Your father has tried so hard to keep her a secret."

It was true.

"It was a surprise," Cody said. "A big surprise."

"I'm glad you're pleased."

He was surprised that his mother was so
cheerful about it. What made her think he was
pleased?

"I don't know if I'm ready for mm . . .
mmm . . . mmm . . ." He couldn't even say
the word *marriage*. "For that," he said instead.

"Well, your father said you weren't respon-
sible enough but I said you were."

"I am?" Cody's mouth dropped open in
surprise. "I'm only nine. Remember my report card. I got a check minus on *Assumes and
displays responsibility.*"

"Oh," his mother said. "That was last year.
You've really grown up."

"I also got a check minus on *Stays on task.*"

"That doesn't matter."

"And a check double minus for *Uses time
wisely.*"

"I've been very proud of the way that you

are growing up. Your dad was afraid that you wouldn't be able to take care of Sita by yourself. But I said you could."

"You know, Mom, Dad's a pretty smart guy. I mean maybe we should listen . . ."

"Listen to you! You are showing your responsibility right now! Cody, we know you've been kind of lonely being an only child."

Cody looked at his mother. A brother or sister would have been just fine. But a wife?

"I have Pal," said Cody.

"Pal is so old," said his mother. "He sleeps all the time. We just wanted to do something special for you."

"Ice cream is special," he said.

She laughed. "Silly," she said. "You are such a joker."

She thought for a moment. "Let's not tell your father that you know about Sita. He'll be disappointed. He really wanted to surprise you."

Cody nodded, although he really wanted

to talk to his dad about this, man to man. But . . . his dad usually wasn't much help in those kinds of talks.

In fact he was usually no help at all. He always talked in sayings, like *Time waits for no man,* or *Never put off till tomorrow what you can do today.* Cody never quite understood what he meant.

Cody remembered one time at Christmas when he had opened a gift that he did not want—a red wool hat with a huge pompom on top that his grandmother had knitted for him.

"It's the thought that counts," his father had said.

Cody wished that his grandmother had not thought of a hat that looked like a fuzzy red tomato on top of his head.

Cody sighed. His dad was no help at all.

His mother walked in and began looking through his closet. "Where is your good Sunday shirt? I want to iron it. I want you to look especially nice when the Avanis are here."

Cody sank down in his bed as she pulled the white shirt out of his closet. A pair of good pants and a sports coat followed.

Cody had always hated to wear that shirt and suit, but now he had good reason to hate it—his Sunday suit had just become his wedding suit.

As he lay in bed that night, he said his prayers:

"Now I lay me down to sleep.
I pray the Lord my soul to keep.
If I should die before I wake,
At least I won't have to get married."

Top Ten Things I Hate to Wear

10. Underwear with pictures on it
 9. Belts
 8. The tomato hat with the pompom
 7. *Anything* with a pompom
 6. Itchy sweaters
 5. Shirts with collars
 4. Party hats
 3. Winter coats
 2. Sunday shoes
 1. Wedding suits

Chapter 9

The Adult Kid

Cody woke up before his alarm even went off. One day closer to the big day. He lay back with his head on his pillow and imagined that he was an adult. He felt his chin for whiskers. Nothing.

Yesterday he hadn't thought that he was ready to grow up this fast, but now he didn't know. He would like to be able to do things like stay up late and eat extra dessert without asking. But . . . then there were the clothes. Adults never looked comfortable.

He looked at the clothes hanging on his doorknob. The stiff white shirt. The tie with its little clip on the back. The tan pants and stiff leather shoes.

He got up, put them on, and looked at himself in the mirror. He straightened his tie like he had seen his father do. He looked like an adult! The tie popped off.

Cody took the suit off and put it back on the coat hanger. But that adult feeling stayed with him.

As he walked downstairs, he cleared his throat. It seemed that his voice had deepened.

"Cody, your breakfast is on the table." His mother tiptoed in from the living room. "Be quiet, dear, the Avanis came in late and they're still asleep."

"Yes, dear," he said.

"What?"

"I mean, uh, never fear."

"Can you get your own breakfast?" she asked. "I'm trying to get a few things done before they get up." She hurried out of the kitchen.

Get his own breakfast? Cody looked at the pot of coffee on the counter. He should have a cup. After all he *was* practically a married man.

He chose a coffee cup that said *So many channels, so little time.* On the cup was the picture of a man in front of the TV, changing channels. Today coffee—tomorrow the channel changer.

Cody picked up the glass pitcher from the coffeemaker and carefully poured the coffee into the cup. He stood for a moment and watched the steam spiral up from the cup. The black liquid looked dark and ominous. It looked adult.

Cody held his nose like kids on TV do when they take medicine. He took a sip, then spit the sip back into the cup. It tasted like dirt, or a toxic chemical, or fossil fuel.

He placed the cup carefully on the table.

Maybe he would try again after the wedding.

"Cody, get going or you'll be late," his mother called into the kitchen door as she hurried by. He picked up his book bag. His dad did not carry a book bag. Cody took everything out and put it into an old briefcase that he found in the closet. He added a newspaper then headed for school.

Ms. Harvey gave him a big smile when he walked into the classroom.

He tried to think of something adult to say. Something that would show everyone his new maturity.

"Good morning, Bree," he said. He continued on to his desk and put his briefcase down. He was especially proud that he had remembered the teacher's first name.

P.J. giggled.

Ms. Harvey's eyes got wider. "What did you say?" she asked Cody. Her smile was gone.

Cody took the morning newspaper out of his briefcase and spread it out.

"Good morning, Bree," he said again.

Ms. Harvey walked over and stood beside him. She lowered herself down to his level. She was not smiling.

"Cody, to you I'm Ms. Harvey," she said. "Do you have your homework?"

"I'll fax it over later," Cody said. Being an adult was great after all. He turned to the comics.

Ms. Harvey felt his head. "Cody, do you feel all right? Would you like to go see the nurse?"

"No thanks." Cody folded the newspaper and checked his watch. "Isn't it almost time for my coffee break?"

P.J. giggled again.

Ms. Harvey tapped her foot. "I think it's almost time for your trip to the hall."

"I'll see if I can work it into my schedule at . . . how about, say . . ." Cody checked his watch . . . "four o'clock? I'll send you a memo. I'll—"

Cody didn't finish. Ms. Harvey picked him

up out of his seat by his collar with a speed that was amazing. She looked at him eye level. Adult to adult.

"How about . . . say . . . *now.*"

Cody saw a blur of laughing faces as he was whisked out the door in a most unadult-like fashion.

Top Ten Things I Hate to Hear

10. The drill at the dentist's office
 9. "You're out!"
 8. The sound of the mail truck
 7. "Your fly is unzipped"
 6. "Time's up, pencils down!"
 5. P.J.'s giggle
 4. Kissing noises
 3. The bell at the beginning of school
 2. Snoring
 1. "I think it's time for a trip to the hall."

Chapter 10

My Teacher, Ms. Hulk

Ms. Harvey seemed bigger in the hall. She towered over him like a monster that he had seen on TV. The monster was called the Incredible Hulk.

When the Hulk got mad he would turn from an ordinary man into a large green hulk with glowing red eyes. Ms. Harvey was looking a little green and a little large.

"Now, Cody," she said, "what is the meaning of all of this?" Did her eyes glow?

He suddenly didn't feel like an adult anymore. He didn't care about the extra desserts or staying up late.

"I'm sorry," Cody said. "I thought I was ready to be grown up but now I don't know. In fact I don't even think I want to be a third grader. In fact I think I'd rather be a baby."

Ms. Harvey looked at him for a moment.

"Goo goo," he said.

She smiled.

"Okay, Cody." She slowly turned back into Ms. Harvey from the Hulk. "You don't need to be a baby, just don't grow up too fast."

"I'm trying not to," he said. "Hard."

"Let's try the day again."

They went back into the class.

Cody sat down. This time he did not read the paper. This time he got out his English book.

He checked his watch. One more hour and Sunda would come.

He tried not to think about his problem, but everything that Ms. Harvey said reminded him of Sita and marriage.

"Today we are going to match up subjects and verbs."

Match up?

In an hour they would be matching up more than verbs. They would be matching up *him*.

"Chip," he whispered.

"Huh?"

"You want my baseball card collection?"

"Sure! Why?"

"I don't think I'll be needing it anymore."

He tried to concentrate on the lesson.

"On page twenty-two," Ms. Harvey continued, "we have the linking verbs."

Linking?

Soon he would be linked, too.

"Chip."

"Huh?"

"You want my stuffed animals?"

"Sure! Why?"

"They are kind of babyish."

"I can give them to my sister," Chip said. "You giving away any more stuff?"

Cody thought for a moment.

"Tigger sheets?"

"No thanks."

Cody checked his watch again. Half an hour left.

Ms. Harvey talked on. "Look how they join with the subject."

Join! Link! Match up!

He put his head down for the rest of English.

"Class," Ms. Harvey said in an excited voice that made Cody look up. "Our visitors are here!"

Cody's dad and Sunda walked into the classroom. Sunda was tall and had dark hair. He wore a suit like Cody's dad's.

They were alone. Maybe they had changed their minds. Maybe they weren't bringing a girl after all.

"Clear your desks. We not only have our special visitor, Mr. Avani, Cody's father tells me we also have a surprise visitor waiting out in the hall."

Cody sank down into his seat. Surprise visitor.

His life flashed before his eyes. First the past: The fun times he had in school. Pre-school. Circle time, cutting and pasting, apple juice and graham crackers. Then his life flashed forward—forward to the life he would never have. Summer camp, Little League, hanging around with his friends at Sparky's Roller Rink, making gross noises on camp-outs.

Finally his thoughts settled on his new life—his life as an adult. He realized all the things that he would miss.

Top Ten Things That Adults Never Do

10. Eat the insides of Oreos first
 9. Jump in leaf piles
 8. Having burping contests
 7. Blow spit bubbles
 6. Say "duh"
 5. Step on catsup packets
 4. Fly paper airplanes
 3. Sing Greasy Grimy Gopher Guts
 2. Gross people out
 1. Act like kids

Chapter 11

Sita!

"Cody, would you like to introduce our special guest?"

Cody shook his head. He couldn't move.

"I'll be glad to, then," Ms. Harvey said. "This is Sunda Avani. He is a friend of Cody's father and comes to us from India."

Everyone clapped.

Sunda took a small bow and then began to talk. He showed maps and jewelry and clothes from India.

He unwrapped a long, beautiful piece of fabric.

"This is a sari," he said. "Women in India sometimes wear them." He wrapped the long piece of cloth around Ms. Harvey until it was a dress. The end of the cloth draped over her shoulder. Everyone clapped.

"Colors have meanings in India," Sunda said. "White means sorrow."

"What does red mean?" Angel asked.

"Red means joy," Sunda said. "When women get married, they often wear red."

Cody blinked twice when he heard the word *married*. The sari was red!

Angel raised her hand again. "What does the groom wear?" she asked.

In a traditional Indian wedding," Sunda said, "the groom dresses like a warrior and rides on a beautifully decorated horse."

Cody gasped. The Sunday suit was bad enough.

Sunda held up an Indian game. "This is Snakes and Ladders," he said.

"We have the same game here," Chip said, "but we call it Chutes and Ladders."

"Indian children love this game," said Sunda.

Cody was not thinking about Snakes and Ladders. He was thinking about horses and warriors and the color red.

"Now it is time for a special introduction," said Sunda.

Cody felt his heart beat faster.

"Cody, could you come up front?"

Cody's feet must have heard the order before his brain did, because he found himself rising to his feet and somehow making it to the front of the room.

He stood beside Sunda and stared out at the class.

He thought fondly of his secret admirer. The best thing about a secret admirer was that she was *secret*.

"Now," said Sunda. "We have a special guest that came all the way from India to live with Cody."

Cody gulped.

"Her name is Sita."

Cody closed his eyes.

"And . . . here she is!"

"Awww!" He could hear the class ooing and ahhing. She must be cute.

"Neat!" he heard Chip say.

Finally he opened one eye, then the other, then he smiled.

"Here she is," said Sunda. "Sita!"

Sunda held a small black and gold turtle. The turtle's feet made swimming movements in the air. Its back was covered with beautiful yellow stars.

"She's an Indian Star tortoise."

He put the small turtle into Cody's hands. "She is a very special tortoise," he said. "Look at the stars on her back."

"Sita?" Cody said to the tortoise. He held it up to his face. Sita ducked back into her shell.

"Sita?" he said again.

"Surprise!" said Sunda.

"Sita!" said Cody. He looked at her shell covered with bright yellow stars. She popped her head out and looked at him. He looked at her feet swimming in the air. He looked at her small, shiny black eyes, and it all made sense.

We're bringing Sita for Cody.
She will be a great addition to the family.
He will love her.
We'll bring the necessary license.

They had not brought him a bride, they had brought him a pet!

"Sita's a tortoise," he said. He jumped up and down.

"A tortoise!" he said again. He hugged the little turtle twice.

"Surprised?" his father asked.

Cody smiled and answered, "You'll never know how much."

Top Ten Best Things About Turtles

10. Turtles are cute.

9. Turtles are good listeners.

8. Turtles are easy to care for.

7. Turtles keep you company.

6. Turtles won't ask you to share your dessert.

5. Turtles can't say "gross" when you burp.

4. Turtles don't get mad at you when you talk to other turtles.

3. Turtles won't ever call you immature.

2. Turtles never send valentines.

1. You can't marry a turtle.

Chapter 12

The Secret Admirer

"Hey." P.J. stopped Cody after class. He waited to see if she was going to make a fist this time. She didn't. "I got your valentine."

"Oh?"

"I'm not in like with you either." She smiled at him.

"So that means," Cody said thoughtfully, "if you don't like me and I don't like you then . . ."

"We can be friends," P.J. finished. She turned and hurried back to the crowd of girls waiting at the door.

Cody shook his head. It was all too confusing, and the question remained: Who was the you-know-who? It might be one of those things that you just never figure out, like photosynthesis or electricity or how Santa Claus gets down the chimney.

"Come on," Chip called. They walked down the hall to go home.

"Are you Cody Michaels?" A tall girl stood at the door of the school waiting for Cody and Chip. She looked tall and old—at least a fifth grader.

Her hair was brown and curly. Cody sniffed the air and felt faint. It was the same smell as the valentine.

"Yeah," Cody said.

Chip nudged Cody.

Before she could say anything else, Chip spoke.

"Do you live around here?" he asked.

She nodded.

"Do you have a purple pen?"

She nodded again.

"Do you like bees?"

"I love 'em," she said.

"And stickers?"

"Uh huh."

Chip looked at Cody. Cody looked at Chip. This was it. This had to be the you-know-who.

Cody asked the final question. "Do you dot your *i*'s with hearts?" His voice cracked when he asked it.

"Always," she said. "Did you get a valentine in the mail?"

Cody's mouth dropped open. She was the one!

"He did," Chip said for him.

"You see, I like this boy."

"You do?"

"He's in fifth grade and his name is Michael Cody. When I looked up his address in the school office, I got your address by mistake. See, Michael Cody—Cody Michaels."

Cody's breath came out in a long whoosh.

"Can I get the card back?" she asked. "I want to give it to him."

Cody smiled as he lifted the card out of his briefcase and handed it to the girl.

He wondered about this guy, this Michael Cody. Right now he was probably shooting baskets or riding his bike, unaware that his life was about to be changed.

"Bye." She wiggled her fingers at them.

"Bye," Cody said. He wiggled back.

Cody walked down the street feeling a lightness that he hadn't felt in exactly three days. The sun seemed brighter, the air fresher.

Being nine was great. He had at least two more years before he had to worry about the mailbox or being in like and at least fifteen more years till marriage.

He passed the mail truck without a second thought and hurried home to see Sita.

Top Ten Things That I Love

10. The smell of cookies in the oven
9. Pizza with pineapple on it
8. My parents' hugs
7. Pal
6. Riding my bike through puddles
5. Getting e-mail
4. Saturday mornings
3. Granny and Aunt Helen
2. Valentines
1. Sita

Betsy Duffey is the author of a wide range of fiction for Puffin, including *How to Be Cool in the Third Grade* and *Utterly Yours, Booker Jones*, plus two previous books about Cody: *Hey, New Kid!* and *Virtual Cody*. She lives in Atlanta, Georgia, with her husband and two sons.

Ellen Thompson is the illustrator of *Hey, New Kid!* and *Virtual Cody* and has illustrated more than a hundred children's book jackets. Her work has also appeared in numerous magazines. She lives in Franklin Park, New Jersey.

Double-O Cupid is on the job!

"Recess," Ms. Harvey called.

Everyone got up and hurried out the door. Everyone but Cody. He sat and watched the others leave. He watched very closely like a detective. Double-O Cupid. Softly he hummed the Mission Impossible *theme song, 'da da, da DA, da da.'*

He knew how he could find his secret admirer. All he had to do was check everyone's writing to see who dotted their i's with a happy-face heart.

Cody waited until the sound of Ms. Harvey's feet died away, then Double-O Cupid made his move. He walked quietly to her desk. There was a pile of English papers on the corner of the desk. He began to look through the papers one by one.

"Cody Michaels! What are you doing?"

Ms. Harvey stood in the doorway of the room. . . .

ALSO BY BETSY DUFFEY